CONTENTS

INTRODUCTION

SICK CALL 6

TWO-WHEEL...OR NOT TWO-WHEEL 8

EGGS-TRAVAGANZA 10

STARSTRUCK 12

DIG THIS 14

SOMETHING FISHY 16

THE KEY QUESTION 18

DENTAL WORK 20

STUCK UP 22

FASHION SHOW 24

UNDERCOVER AGENT 26

GOOD NEIGHBOR 28

TO FLY A KITE 30

POP GOES THE WEASEL 32

TURN AROUND, DRIVER 34

FALSE ALARM 36

COAT CHECK 38

THE FATAL SLIP 40

BABY-SITTER 42

DARWIN AND THE RANDAN 44

WORK OF ART 46

JUST A BITE 48

CAW, CAW, CAW 50

CHRISTMAS TREE 52

ANSWERS 54

ABOUT THE CREATORS 62

GET A CLUE

25 PICTURE MYSTERIES

By Lawrence Treat

Illustrated by Paul Karasik

Cover illustrations by Mary Bono

Grosset & Dunlap • New York

INTRODUCTION

As everybody knows, no two things or people are exactly alike. They can come close, but never exactly. And this fact, very simply, is the key to *Get a Clue*. Still, finding the difference between two things, and the difference that that difference makes, isn't always easy.

Each puzzle in this book poses a mystery for you to solve—a mystery based on two pictures with a difference for you to spot. The best advice I can give you is to look carefully. There is always a difference, maybe several. And there is always a logical explanation for everything you see, or maybe fail to see.

Like any good detective, your job will be to build a case based on the evidence before you. Good luck. And remember, like any good puzzle-solver, you can always check your answers in the back of the book.

Lawrence Treat

SICK CALL

Binky Bateman hated the second Saturday of every month because that was when the family visited Aunt Viola and Uncle George. All those wet kisses from Aunt Viola, and Uncle George's bad breath. Yuck! But this Saturday, Binky woke up sick and called her mother.

Binky's mom brought Binky into the bathroom and took out the thermometer, as shown in Drawing **A**. Then the phone rang, and

Mrs. Bateman left to answer it. When she returned, in Drawing **B**, and checked Binky's temperature, the thermometer read one hundred and four.

Binky's mom studied it carefully, then said, "Binky, get dressed this instant and get ready to go."

Why did she force such an apparently sick girl to go visiting?

TWO-WHEEL...OR NOT TWO-WHEEL

The Junkos, the Smiths, and the Feuders lived at the dead end of a dead-end road. The three families shared a small toolshed, which they kept locked to protect their possessions: their lawn mowers, their garden tools, and Jon-Jon Feuder's brand-new thirty-seven-speed bike.

The three kids were friends, but they had their differences, too. Kiki Junko was the center on the girls' basketball team. Shorty Smith was the center on the football team. And Jon-Jon, although no great athlete, was the center of his parents' universe.

B

Drawing **A** shows Jon-Jon showing off his new bike for the sixty-fifth time that week. Drawing **B** shows the same scene the next day, after someone had apparently taken it for a ride....

Since only the three families had keys to the toolshed, Jon-Jon figured that either Kiki or Shorty must have been the culprit.

Which one would you accuse if you were Jon-Jon?

EGGS-TRAVAGANZA

It was a family tradition that every Easter, General Faraway invited the entire Faraway clan to celebrate the holiday at his estate. This meant getting up at dawn, eating a huge breakfast, then having every Faraway under the age of thirteen hunt for Easter eggs. The rules were simple. The older children (those over the age of 13) would hide the eggs in the general's study, one for every egg hunter. Then the younger children would hunt.

During the hunt, the general would sit in his favorite chair and wait for the

grown-ups in the family to ask him how his health was and to hear the history of the chair. Sometimes the general claimed it had belonged to General George Washington. Other times he said it was General Robert E. Lee's. But the point was that only he, General Faraway, was good enough to sit in it.

Drawing **A** shows the study before the Easter eggs were hidden. Drawing **B** shows the general seated in his chair as the hunt is about to begin. Can you find all five eggs before the children do?

STARSTRUCK

Kitty Kicklekin had a problem. Saturday afternoon, Lionel Limpet, the movie star on whom Kitty had a deep and desperate crush, was on location just a few blocks away. She *had* to get his autograph. Her mother, however, was far more concerned with Kitty's grades than her starstruck love life, and insisted that Kitty spend the afternoon studying for her final exams while the rest of the family went off to her brother Kip's Little League ball game. Only Grandpa opted out of going along. "Kids," he said. "What do they

know about baseball?" So he said he'd stick around to make sure Kitty stayed home and studied.

Drawing **A** shows Kitty after the Kicklekins left for the ball game. Drawing **B** shows her hours later, just before they returned and Kitty's mother praised her for being such a good girl. Kip, meanwhile, burst out laughing.

Why?

DIG THIS

When Jerry was three, he wanted to be a truck. When he was four, he could name all the trucks on the road. When he was five, he got the dump truck of his dreams for his birthday, along with strict instructions from his mother never to dig around the house, especially not in her flower garden.

Drawing **A** shows Jerry playing with his truck, while his dog, Nap, naps in the background. Drawing **B** shows Jerry an hour later, when his mother accused him of digging up that big hole in her garden.

"It wasn't me," Jerry said. "It must have been Nap. Silly dog."

Was it?

Angelina hated fish. She hated angelfish and bass and carp and dace and eel and flounder and grouper and haddock, and all the rest of the alphabet. So when she sat down to dinner Friday night and discovered a poached pompano staring up at her from her plate, she turned up her nose, which she was very good at.

Drawing **A** shows Angelina sulking after her mother told her, "You will sit here until you're done," and left the room.

Drawing **B** shows Angelina after her mother returned. "Did you eat it all up?" her mother asked.

Did she?

THE KEY QUESTION

A

Kim was used to coming home and letting himself in after school when his parents worked late, and they'd given him a house key on a big golf-ball key chain for that purpose.

Drawing **A** shows Kim one sunny afternoon, playing with the cat on the back porch before he let himself inside. It was then that Kim remembered

he'd forgotten to get the mail, and he walked around to the front of the house to check the mailbox.

Drawing **B** shows Kim returning, shocked to discover that his golf-ball key chain and, more importantly, his key were gone.

Can you find it?

DENTAL WORK

Margaret was lucky. Every day, her father picked her up at school and they chatted peacefully as he drove her home. This day, however, Margaret was unlucky. When her dad pulled into the driveway, he broke the bad news. She had a dental appointment the next morning.

"I'm not going!" Margaret declared. But her dad insisted.

Drawing **A** shows him getting out of the car, explaining to an angry Margaret that they will be leaving at 8 a.m. sharp. Drawing **B** shows her a few minutes later, this time smiling.

Why?

STUCK UP

"I need a tune-up, and right this instant!" Mrs. Penn Warrington III told the mechanic, Mr. Lever. "And keep that brat of yours away from my car!"

Mrs. Penn Warrington III was well known in the community for her impatience and her dislike of children, but people put up with her because of her money.

Drawing **A** shows Mr. Lever dashing off to answer the phone before starting work on Mrs. Penn Warrington's car. His son, little Joe Lever Jr., is beside him.

Drawing **B** shows Mr. Lever returning to find Mrs. Penn Warrington in a most undignified position.

How did she get stuck up?

FASHION SHOW

Mrs. Lily Prettyman, a former Miss Chicago, had a fabulous collection of clothes, and loved to shop for more. Drawing **A** shows her in her room before a day-long shopping trip, saying good-bye to her daughter, Dawn.

Drawing **B** shows the room when Lily returned early and found one of her best cocktail dresses ripped. "I don't know how it happened!" Dawn said. But Lily did.

Do you?

UNDERCOVER AGENT

Mrs. Spandulex was a loving mother and felt it important that her son Jefferson should get a good night's sleep. Drawing **A** shows her checking on him at 8:00 p.m. "Now Jefferson," she told him, "put out that light and go to sleep. Your space mysteries can wait till tomorrow."

Drawing **B** shows Mrs. Spandulex returning to Jefferson's room a little while later. "I could have sworn I heard a sound," she said. "But I guess it was nothing. I'm sorry if I woke you."

Do you think she did?

GOOD NEIGHBOR

Nobody knew who had cleaned up mean Old Man Cotton's run-down house while he was spending the Christmas holidays with his twin sister in Ohio. But he had three neighbors with the time and skill to make repairs—namely, Rip Sawyer, Rusty Hooks, and Mick Tinker. Still, no one would confess to the good deed for fear of Old Man Cotton's wrath and possible charges of trespassing. So the identity of the good Samaritan remained a mystery until by chance, Vinny Vansant figured it out.

Like most kids in town, Vinny always went past Old Man Cotton's house without stopping, because if Old Man Cotton caught you he would sic his dog on you. Then one day on a dare, Vinny stopped and did a handstand outside Old Man Cotton's front gate. And that's when it dawned on him who the good neighbor must be.

Drawing **A** shows the Cotton house before repairs. Drawing **B** shows it the day Vinny stood on his head. Can you figure out who fixed up the place?

TO FLY A KITE

Willy could do everything. He could pitch. He could skateboard. He could Rollerblade. But being a city boy, he'd never had the chance to fly a kite. His chance came when he went to visit his cousin, Billy, in the country.

"Like this?" Willy asked Billy as he tried to launch his first kite, as shown in Drawing **A**.

"Not exactly," Billy replied, and gave Willy some advice, which he took in Drawing **B**. What was Billy's advice?

POP GOES THE WEASEL

Everybody in Mrs. Tatch's eighth-grade class was familiar with her solid gold weasel brooch—though why a weasel, nobody knew. Even her son, Durgin, who was in the seventh grade, wasn't sure exactly what it meant. All he knew was that his mother loved it more than any other piece of jewelry, that she wore it every day, and that she kept it by her bedside when she went to sleep.

Drawing **A** shows Mrs. Tatch switching off her bedside light late one evening, after putting the brooch on the bedside table. Drawing **B** shows Mrs. Tatch reaching for her brooch the next morning and discovering it missing.

Who stole it?

TURN AROUND, DRIVER

A

When the Cruikshank family went to Europe for spring vacation, Mom saw to it that everything was done ahead of time in a neat and orderly fashion. The day before they left, she oversaw little Evelyn's packing, and did the same for Roger Junior. Dad, of course, left all of his packing to Mom as he always did.

Drawing **A** shows the Cruikshank house on the morning of their departure, after they stepped out to take a taxi to the airport. They had gone about a mile when Mrs. Cruikshank said, "Turn around, Driver. I want to check on something."

Drawing **B** shows the house after Mrs. Cruikshank had gone back and left for a second time, this time with her mind at rest. Why?

FALSE ALARM

Fancy loved to stay up late reading horse books, but it always made waking up in the morning hard. This night, though, her mother warned her: "I'm picking up your Aunt Millie at the airport at six o'clock tomorrow morning, and I want you up and dressed by the time we get back."

Drawing **A** shows Fancy that night after her mother plugged in an alarm clock and set it to wake Fancy at 6 a.m.

Drawing **B** shows Fancy still asleep at 8 the next morning, just before her mother walked in with Aunt Millie in tow.

"I guess the alarm never went off," Fancy said after her mother woke her up. "I must have tripped over the cord when I went to the bathroom during the night and yanked it out of the outlet."

Do you believe her?

COAT CHECK

Now and then, Andy earned extra money by checking coats during lectures at the local university. Drawing **A** shows Andy checking the coat of a man with a mustache before the start of a lecture by FBI agent Olivia Ovilia. When all the coats were checked, Andy left his post to get a drink of water.

When he returned, in Drawing **B**, he found the same man putting on a coat by himself. "You weren't here," the man said. "But don't worry about losing your job. I won't tell."

"No," said Andy. "But I will."

What crime did he have to report?

THE FATAL SLIP

No one liked doing exercises before the start of classes, especially Nippy Van Hosen. But Mr. Torrant, the science teacher, was convinced that it woke up students' brains—if they had any.

Drawing **A** shows Nippy leaving class one day. Drawing **B** shows him hobbling in on crutches the next morning. "I sprained my ankle slipping

off my skateboard," Nippy said. "It hurt a lot, but my mom fixed me up like this. She says education is the most important thing in the world, and so I have to go to school. But I guess I'll have to skip those morning exercises for a while, won't I, Mr. Torrant?"

Should Mr. Torrant excuse Nippy?

BABY-SITTER

Benjy Tuttle's baby-sitter, Loni, had been warned not to sneak any more food from the Tuttles' fridge, and had promised not to do it again.

Drawing **A** shows Benjy checking the fridge before Loni came. Drawing **B** shows his mom checking it when she got home.

Did Loni keep her promise?

DARWIN AND THE RANDAN

Uncle Evan was a seafaring man clear down to his boots, which squeaked even on dry land. And to anyone who'd listen, Uncle Evan would explain that his favorite boat wasn't a rowboat or a dory or a dinghy or a skiff or a gig or a punt or a shallop or a shell. It was a randan, which is made for three oarsmen handling four oars.

Uncle Evan's only rule was that nobody should take his randan out without him, and Drawing **A** shows him repeating the rules to his nephew, Darwin, before going off to lunch. Drawing **B** shows the dock several hours later when Uncle Evan returned.

Did Darwin obey the rule?

WORK OF ART

Lennie Westerhouse spent most of his time in class making sketches of his teacher, Mr. Richards, instead of listening to him. And the sketches were not flattering. Mr. Richards, however, had a hunch that Lennie was up to no good, and was determined to catch him in the act. But the rest of the class loved Lennie's drawings and did all they could to help him out.

Drawing **A** shows Lennie's classroom during one of Mr. Richards's famous pop quizzes, as he's about to catch Lennie with sketch #47, and as his classmates try to save him by staging a noisy diversion.

Drawing **B** shows the room after Mr. Richards has calmed the class and returned to deal with Lennie. Little does Mr. Richards know there'll be no evidence to be found. What did Lennie do to keep from being caught?

JUST A BITE

Mrs. Fruitcake was famous for her gingerbread houses. People said they looked good enough to eat, and they were. She was making one for the County Fair when she ran out of colored icing for the roof. "I have to go to the store," she told her son Ralph. "Watch the gingerbread and make sure that Gyp doesn't eat it!"

Drawing **A** shows Ralph and his dog, Gyp, in the kitchen after Mrs. Fruitcake had left them. Drawing **B** shows how they looked when she returned. "The phone rang," Ralph said, "and I went to answer it. I guess Gyp took a bite out of the wall while I was gone."

Do you believe him?

CAW, CAW, CAW

One of the first things the Byrds noticed when they moved into the beach house for the month of August was the bird feeder attached to the sliding glass door. It was made for small birds, and yet a big crow kept trying to peck at the seeds.

Robin, the youngest of the Byrd family, was smitten with the crow. "That's one smart bird!" he said. "Wait and see. I'm going to feed him every day and teach him tricks."

Drawing **A** shows the crow the first time Robin saw it. Drawing **B** shows the same scene at the end of the month, when Robin gathered his family together to exhibit his trained crow. "First I'll make him hover like a hummingbird," Robin said.

But instead of performing, the crow ignored him.

Why?

CHRISTMAS TREE

For generations the McPushkins had used the same Christmas tree ornaments. Some of them dated back to colonial times, but by far the most valuable items were blown-glass ornaments from faraway Venice. The glass fruits were so perfectly made that birds could mistake them for the real thing and shatter them by pecking away. But because they were kept in the attic and taken out only once a year, the glass fruits survived. An antique dealer who saw them had offered Mr. McPushkin $2,000 just for one, but the ornaments were not for sale.

Drawing **A** shows the tree as Mrs. Yolanda McPushkin finished hanging the precious decorations. Drawing **B** shows Mr. Ali McPushkin making the final inspection on Christmas Eve. He had already noticed his son admiring the ornaments, and now he exploded in anger. "Come here, Manfred!" he bellowed. "I want a word with you!"

What did Mr. McPushkin notice, and why was he so angry?

ANSWERS

SICK CALL (pages 6-7)

Binky's mother knew that if Binky's temperature were one hundred and four, she would have been too sick to walk to the bathroom. She also noticed the sink faucet, which had somehow started to leak while she was on the phone. That's when she realized that Binky must have turned on the hot water and held the thermometer under it until it reached one hundred and four, then quickly turned off the faucet, but left the water dripping.

Smart girl, Binky, but even smarter mother.

TWO-WHEEL...OR NOT TWO-WHEEL (pages 8-9)

Kiki. She is tall (5'10 1/2" to be exact), and Shorty was nicknamed "Shorty" for a very good reason. Whoever wrecked the bike raised the seat, which only a tall person would have to do. Consequently, Kiki is the guilty party.

After Jon-Jon accused Kiki, the Junkos and the Feuders never spoke to each other again. Eventually, the Junkos moved away to another dead-end road and bought Jon-Jon a new bike with an immovable seat. But it was too high.

EGGS-TRAVAGANZA (pages 10-11)

Four eggs are clearly visible:
> One in the cabinet in the wine glass
> One on the windowsill behind the curtain
> One on the floor beside the fire tools
> One in the fruit bowl

And the fifth egg? It is under General Faraway, who sat down without realizing that the egg was there and that it was still raw.

As one junior Faraway whispered to another, "The general lied when he said there were five eggs. Actually there are only four—and an omelet."

The general overheard the remark and was not pleased.

STARSTRUCK (pages 12-13)

Kip, whose eye level was not much higher than Kitty's boots, noticed what nobody else had: that Kitty's boots had been unlaced and retied. And Kip had been around Kitty long enough to know she'd never mess up a perfect outfit unless she absolutely had to. Kitty had taken her boots off for a reason and had put them back on in a hurry. Her reason must have been to sneak out and back without waking Grandpa.

But, Kip knew better than to tell on Kitty. Instead, he made her promise to take him to the movies. Kitty gratefully granted his wish and took him to a show the next Saturday. To Kip's disgust, it was a Lionel Limpet film. And what kind of present was that?

DIG THIS (pages 14-15)

No. Judging by the absence of any soil other than the pile in Jerry's truck and the small amount next to the neat hole, Jerry dug that hole himself. A dog would have scattered the soil in a wide arc and left the hole irregular, but the sides of this hole are smooth and straight, as they would be if made by a boy with a shovel like the one in Jerry's pail.

This was obvious to Jerry's mother, who promptly put the dump truck out of commission until further notice.

SOMETHING FISHY (pages 16-17)

No. The cat did. The cat in Drawing **B** is licking its paws, which cats often do after they finish eating. Since cats love fish, and Angelina didn't, the cat and she must have come to an unspoken agreement. The cat could have the fish, and Angelina could have the bones.

Her mother, however, guessed what Angelina had done, and they had a long talk about the evils of lying. Afterwards, Angelina reluctantly agreed to a taste of pompano, which has the reputation of being the most delicious of all fish. And probably because it is so expensive, Angelina found she loved it. From then on, whenever her mother made fish for dinner, they pretended it was pompano, and Angelina ate every bite.

The only loser was the cat.

THE KEY QUESTION (pages 18-19)

It's in the watering can, as shown by the higher level of water in Drawing **B**, and the drops of water around it. These clues suggest that the cat thought the key chain a wonderful toy, and batted it off the porch and into the watering can while Kim was gone.

DENTAL WORK (pages 20-21)

Margaret was smiling because she had discovered how to avoid going to the dentist. If she turned on the headlights and they stayed on all night, they would drain the car's battery so it couldn't start the next day. Unfortunately, her plan was foiled when her dad took out the garbage around 10:30 that night, noticed the lights on, and turned them off. Bright and early the next morning, he had the car ready and waiting for Margaret.

After the dentist told her she should be a tooth model, however, Margaret perked up, and always looked forward to dental visits.

STUCK UP (pages 22-23)

Little Joe had ideas on how to get back at Mrs. Penn Warrington III while his dad was on the phone. He was too small to reach the lever for the hydraulic car lift without standing on something, so instead he picked up the coat hanger he saw lying on the ground, bent it, and used it to hook the lever that raised the car. And up the lady went.

Once back down, she was still stuck up.

FASHION SHOW (pages 24-25)

Being a former model, as well as a beauty queen, made Lily aware of details in clothing. In Drawing **B**, Dawn's T-shirt tag is showing beneath her ponytail. She had been trying on her mother's dresses and accidentally tore one. When her mother came home early, Dawn barely had time to slip her T-shirt back on, inside out.

No allowance for a month!

UNDERCOVER AGENT (pages 26-27)

No, Mrs. Spandulex did not wake Jefferson. The flashlight missing from his nightstand in Drawing **B** and the disappearance of the book he was reading point instead to the fact that Jefferson was reading by flashlight under his covers just before Mrs. Spandulex came in. Lucky for him, she never picked up on the clues, and his cover was never blown.

GOOD NEIGHBOR (pages 28-29)

Mick Tinker proudly signed his handiwork by carving his initials upside down on the cap of Old Man Cotton's fence post. Vinny saw the initials clearly when he was standing on his head, which just goes to show how useful a useless talent such as standing on one's head can be.

TO FLY A KITE (pages 30-31)

"The only way to launch a kite," Billy told Willy, "is to run and pull it into the wind."

The way the trees are bending and the way the birds are facing in Drawings **A** and **B** show that the wind is blowing to the left, which means the only way for Willy to get his kite into the air is to run to the right and into the wind.

POP GOES THE WEASEL (pages 32-33)

Durgin. The fact that Mrs. Tatch's faithful dog, Pop, did not get up and bark during the night proves that the brooch must have been taken by someone he trusted. Therefore, Durgin. The fact that the sliding door was ajar was simply a diversion staged by Durgin to throw his mother off his trail.

Faced with the evidence, Durgin confessed. "But Mom," he said, "Rip Ripper made me do it! He said I'd never see the eighth grade if I didn't steal your brooch for him. So I did."

Although disappointed in her son, Mrs. Tatch realized that the real culprit here was Rip Ripper, and she reported him to the proper authorities.

TURN AROUND, DRIVER (pages 34-35)

Mrs. Cruikshank went back to lock the sliding glass door, as you can see by the changed position of the latch. "I don't know how I could have forgotten something so important," Mrs. Cruikshank said to herself. But that was nothing compared to the shock she felt when they arrived in Paris and discovered that little Evelyn had repacked her suitcase with dolls only. Poor Mrs. Cruikshank!

FALSE ALARM (pages 36-37)

No. Although the alarm is pulled out of the outlet, and the clock does read four o'clock, the time when Fancy supposedly went to the bathroom during the night, the evidence is not convincing. Had Fancy tripped on the cord on her way to the bathroom, as she claimed, the clock on the edge of the bookshelf would have fallen to the floor, or at least been moved. Also, she neglected to push the chair back after she moved it aside to reach the socket.

Hard-working girl, Fancy, but no horse sense.

COAT CHECK (pages 38-39)

Andy noticed that the coat the man had taken was unlike the one he had checked, in one important detail. The coat he had taken had buttons on the left instead of on the right, which meant that it was a woman's coat, and not a man's.

Furthermore, this particular coat belonged to Olivia Ovilia, and had important classified documents sewn into its lining.

Thanks to Andy, the man was discovered to be a spy and was immediately arrested. For his quick thinking, Andy hoped to get a thank-you call from the President, which didn't happen. But it could have, couldn't it?

THE FATAL SLIP (pages 40-41)

No, Nippy is faking. The purpose of a crutch is to take the weight off an injured leg or foot. Nippy is holding his crutch on the wrong side. Mr. Torrant was even more convinced that students needed exercise to wake up their brains, and that Nippy needed a double dose.

BABY-SITTER (pages 42-43)

No. The five-layer cake in Drawing **A** is a four-layer cake in Drawing **B**, proving not only that Loni has a sweet tooth, but that she is deft with kitchen utensils. Although some day she hoped to be a top pastry chef, for the present, Loni's talent has cost her her job.

Benjy hoped his next sitter wouldn't have a sweet tooth.

DARWIN AND THE RANDAN (pages 44-45)

No. Darwin not only broke Uncle Evan's rule, he broke his heart. Although Darwin was careful to put the oars and life preservers back exactly as he found them, he failed to notice how the line was tied to its post. Uncle Evan always tied a sailor's knot (a double hitch). But the only knot Darwin knew was the one he used to tie his shoes.

WORK OF ART (pages 46-47)

Lennie might not have been a great scholar, but he was quick-witted. While his friends distracted Mr. Richards, Lennie managed to fold his drawing into a paper airplane and send it through the open window beside his desk. Part of the flying artwork can still be seen, carried off by a passing breeze.

Pleased with his success, Lennie turned his attention back to the test and passed with flying colors.

JUST A BITE (pages 48-49)

No, Ralph's story cannot be true. The shape of the bite is large and roundish, like the shape of Ralph's mouth, not that of his dog (who would have gobbled up the whole piece). Besides, to get at the gingerbread, Gyp would have knocked over the things in front of the pan. All Ralph had to do was reach over them. Thus, Mrs. Fruitcake knew that Ralph had taken the bite, and she chewed him out.

CAW, CAW, CAW (pages 50-51)

The crow paid no attention to Robin because it was not the bird that Robin had been training. The crow in Drawing **A** has a missing claw on its left foot. The crow in Drawing **B** has all its claws. Robin's hard work was not in vain, however. About an hour later, the trained crow appeared and Robin proved to his family how much a crow without a toe can know.

CHRISTMAS TREE (pages 52-53)

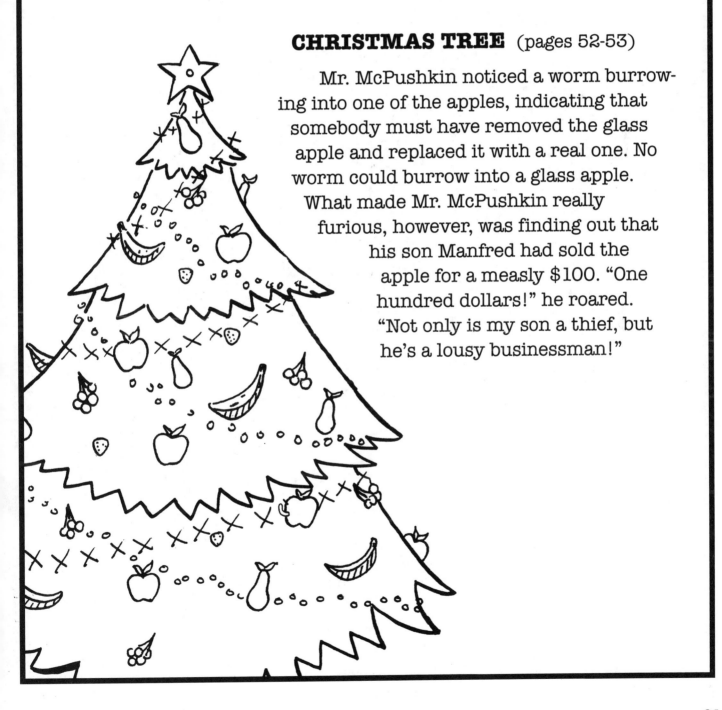

Mr. McPushkin noticed a worm burrowing into one of the apples, indicating that somebody must have removed the glass apple and replaced it with a real one. No worm could burrow into a glass apple. What made Mr. McPushkin really furious, however, was finding out that his son Manfred had sold the apple for a measly $100. "One hundred dollars!" he roared. "Not only is my son a thief, but he's a lousy businessman!"

ABOUT THE CREATORS

Lawrence Treat, novelist and short story writer, is a two-time recipient of the Edgar Allan Poe Award, the highest honor in the field of mystery writing. He was also a prize winner at the Crime Writers' International Short Story Contest, held in Stockholm, Sweden, in 1981, and received a ceremonial dagger in Tokyo from the Mystery Writers of Japan. A founder and past president of the Mystery Writers of America, Mr. Treat is the originator of the picture-mystery puzzle, many of which also appear in his best-selling series *Crime and Puzzlement*. He lives on Martha's Vineyard with his wife, artist Rose Treat.

Paul Karasik has illustrated two of Mr. Treat's previous picture-mystery puzzle books. He is a former associate editor of *Raw Magazine*, the international comics review. With artist David Mazzuccelli, he adapted Paul Auster's *City of Glass* into a graphic novel that has been translated into four languages. He, too, lives on Martha's Vineyard with his family.

Drawing **A** shows Mr. Treat and Mr. Karasik beginning work on *Get a Clue*. Drawing **B** shows them with just one puzzle left to do. See if you can deduce why they almost could not finish.

Answer: They nearly ran out of ink!